I wish you **courage** and *strength*, for the magic begins at the end of your comfort zone.

I wish you *imagination* and *creativity*, for the world is a blank canvas to paint your masterpiece.

I wish you *adventure*
and *curiosity*, to go
where there is no path
and leave a trail.

I wish you *health* and *well-being*, for they are worth more than all the riches in the world.

I wish you *peace* and *tranquility*, to
listen to the birds and gaze at the stars.

I wish you *knowledge* and *wisdom*, for they are the foundations of a successful life.

I wish you *grit* and *resilience*, to never ever give up.

I wish you *success*
and *prosperity*, to
trust yourself and your
ability to succeed.

I wish you *luck* and
opportunity, for
the more you try, the
luckier you get.

I wish you *faith* and *hope*, to
believe everything will be all right.

I wish you *family* and
friendships, for they
are life's greatest sources
of happiness.

I wish you *joy* and *laughter*, to laugh long and loud until you gasp for breath.

I wish you *kindness* and *generosity*, for no act of kindness is ever wasted, no matter how small.

I wish you *love* and **affection**, to fill your beautiful heart with an ocean of joy.

I wish you all those wonderful things,
but most of all . . .

I wish you
happiness!

Can You Spot the Famous People?

No matter what obstacles you face, believe in yourself and all that you are—
just like these famous people did. Can you spot all five in the book?

Can you spot a young Neil Armstrong?

Neil is a famous astronaut who became the first person to walk on the
moon in 1969. Before that, he was an experimental research test pilot,
which is a very dangerous job.

Can you spot a young Katherine Johnson?

Katherine is a mathematician whose calculations helped send the
Apollo 11 rocket carrying Neil Armstrong and his fellow astronauts to
the moon.

Can you spot a young Amelia Earhart?

Amelia was the first female aviator to fly solo across the Atlantic
Ocean. She helped to create The Ninety-Nines, an international
organization of women pilots.

Can you spot a young J. K. Rowling?

Twelve publishers rejected Joanne's first book. She had to wait a year
before her book was finally published. Her Harry Potter books went on
to become the best-selling book series in history.

Can you spot a young Alexander Selkirk?

Alexander famously spent four years as a castaway on an uninhabited
island. His survival story inspired Daniel Defoe's Robinson Crusoe,
often credited as the first English novel, published in 1719.

Can You Spot the Dogs?

There are seventeen dogs and one cat in the book. Can you spot them all?

Beagle	Cavalier King Charles Spaniel	Dalmatian
French Bulldog	German Shepherd	Golden Retriever
Jack Russell Terrier	Labrador Retriever	Maltese
Pomeranian	Poodle	Pug
Saint Bernard	Shiba Inu	Siamese Cat
Welsh Corgi	West Highland Terrier	Yorkshire Terrier

We hope you enjoyed the book.
Your opinion matters. Please leave a review on Amazon and PiccoPuppy.com.
Tell others why you enjoyed this book. Thank you.

Hardcover · Personalized · Bilingual

I Wish You Happiness is available as a 10x10 inch jacketed hardcover, and personalized, bilingual, French, German, Italian, and Spanish editions.

A thoughtful gift for baby showers, birthdays, and graduations. Available on Amazon, PiccoPuppy.com, and in bookstores.

Michael Wong is an award-winning children's author. He is passionate about creating empowering, diverse, and inclusive books for children. Michael lives with his wife and two children in Sydney, Australia.

Ann Baratashvili is an illustrator and concept artist. She won first prize in the 2009 DeviantArt/Wacom "Bring Your Vision to Life: Dreams" contest. Ann lives with her husband and son in Tbilisi, Georgia.

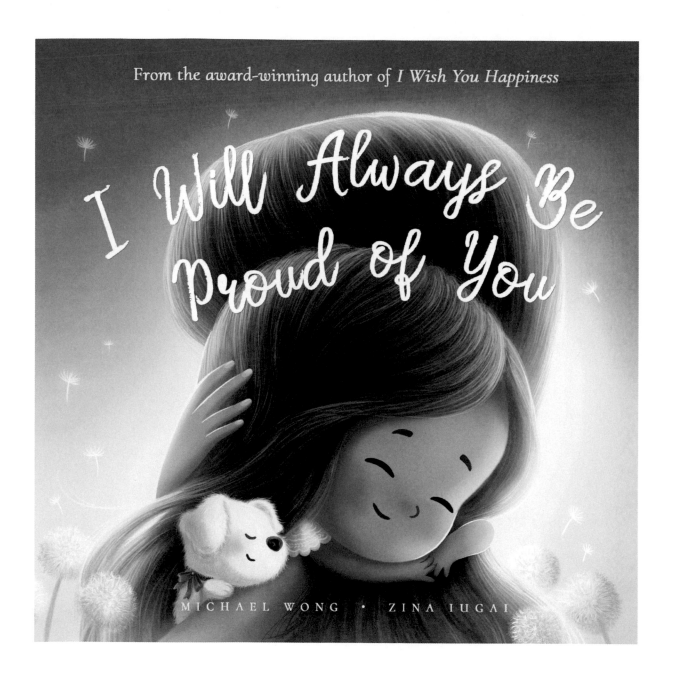

From the award-winning author of *I Wish You Happiness*

I Will Always Be Proud of You

MICHAEL WONG · ZINA IUGAI

I Will Always Be Proud of You is the follow-up to *I Wish You Happiness*.
Available on Amazon and PiccoPuppy.com.

Made in United States
Orlando, FL
22 August 2022